SUPER SLEUTH

Brains, our new crime-lab officer, peered at the suspicious note. He happened to turn the paper over.

"Hey! Now this **is** interesting!"

He was staring at a scribble on the back.

"Oh, forget the scribble!" said McGurk. "What about the handwriting?"

"No, this is very important!" said Brains. "This 'scribble' is part of a burglar-alarm circuit. Whoever wrote the note sent along a plan of the alarm system. Probably so his accomplice would know just how to put it out of action during the robbery."

We stared at the scribble, and at Brains. McGurk's eyes were shining. Now we were getting somewhere!

A McGURK MYSTERY #6

The Case of the Secret Scribbler

by E.W. Hildick

Illustrated by Lisl Weil

AN ARCHWAY PAPERBACK
POCKET BOOKS • NEW YORK

POCKET BOOKS, a Simon & Schuster division of
GULF & WESTERN CORPORATION
1230 Avenue of the Americas, New York, N.Y. 10020

ISBN: 0-671-56014-X

First Pocket Books printing December, 1979

10 9 8 7 6 5 4 3 2 1

Trademarks registered in the United States and other countries.

Printed in the U.S.A.

Contents

The Case of the Secret Scribbler

1

The Scrap of Paper

"I think we've hit on a *really* big case this time!" said McGurk. "Tell 'em, Joey."

His eyes were glowing a bright go-ahead green. I suddenly began to feel doubtful. Sure, I was the one who'd found the scrap of paper that *looked* like a clue to a big crime. But I

1

didn't feel half as positive about it as McGurk. So this big buildup he'd given me only made me more afraid than ever of disappointing the others.

I looked around the table. We were in McGurk's basement, our headquarters. All the members of the McGurk Organization were present except one. Wanda Grieg and Willie Sandowsky had come at once in answer to McGurk's call. It was a dull rainy morning and they were only too glad of something to do, I guess. I mean, it certainly wasn't anything special that McGurk had said on the phone. Naturally, he'd told them it was something urgent:

"Top priority! We've just had word of a really big crime! Get moving!"

But he was always saying things like that.

Wanda glanced at the empty chair. She'd gotten pretty wet coming over to McGurk's. Her long blond hair was hanging down in dark rattails. She looked all set to be very critical.

"How about Brains?" she said. "Shouldn't we wait for him? If it's as big a crime as all *that,* maybe we'll need to use his crime lab."

Brains Bellingham was our newest member. Having only just turned ten, he wasn't quite as old as the rest of us, and for a long time we'd resisted letting him join the Organization. But

2

he was so brilliant with scientific things—especially in The Case of the Invisible Dog—that we finally gave in, a couple of weeks before all this happened.

McGurk shook his head.

"Brains couldn't make it. He's been grounded. He has to stay home this morning and talk to an insurance investigator."

This piece of news seemed to interest Wanda and Willie much more than the crime McGurk had mentioned.

"Insurance investigator?" said Wanda. "Why?"

"To explain about a flood," I said.

"In their yard?" asked Willie. His hair had gotten all spiky from the rain—so that what with that and the long sharp nose of his he reminded me somehow of the Statue of Liberty. "I didn't know it had rained *that* hard."

"No," I said. "In their bathroom. Seems that Brains was experimenting with one of his fancy devices. An electronic flood warning. When the water in the tub rose to a certain level it was supposed to trigger a warning on the radio in his room. A burst of interference or something."

"Only it didn't work," said McGurk, impatiently. "And the first warning anyone got was when the water began splashing through the kitchen ceiling, right on his mother's head. . . . Hey, come on, Joey! Forget Brains and his domestic problems. Tell 'em about the clue you found."

So I began.

I was hard work at first, with Wanda and Willie still being more interested in Brains's flood than my story about the library book.

"It was my father's really," I explained. "A book about Morocco. He's thinking we might take a trip there next year and—"

"Is it going to cost a lot?" Willie asked.

"What—the trip?"

"No. The damage. You know. To the Bellinghams' bathroom and kitchen."

A growl came from the head of the table. McGurk's hair seemed to catch fire and grow two shades redder as he leaned forward under the light.

"Officer Sandowsky, I order you to keep quiet! Joey—get to the clue. Tell them what you found in the library book. *Show* it to them. Now!"

"Well"—I fumbled in one of the boxes we use as files, the box labeled CLUES—"it was this scrap of paper."

I laid it on the table. It was about five inches by four inches, slightly ragged along two edges, as if it had been torn from a larger sheet. And the side I showed them first was the one with the scribble. Like this:

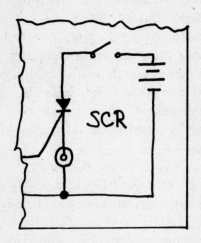

"Huh! That's just some old doodling!" said Willie. "What's *that* got to do with a crime?"

"Maybe McGurk thinks scribbling *is* a crime," said Wanda, giving her hair a toss in McGurk's direction and spraying him with drops of water.

"Hey, yeah!" said Willie—and he suddenly looked so solemn it was impossible to tell if he was kidding. "Maybe it's a Mastermind Scribbler at work. Look—he's even signed it. SCR for Scribbler.''

"Or SCR for SECRET," said Wanda. "Or both. Is that it, McGurk? We're on the track of a *Secret* Scribbler? The very worst kind?" She stopped grinning. She began to look mad. "You mean you've dragged us over here, in the pouring rain, just for this? I mean, it isn't as if the person had done his scribbling on the pages of the book. That *might* be called a crime. But this—"

McGurk grinned as he interrupted. He was really enjoying this.

"Show 'em the other side, Joey."

Then all at once I began to enjoy it, too. Leaving the scrap where it was, I said:

"Well, first let me explain that there seemed to be *nothing* on the other side. But then I noticed that someone must have been writing something on another piece of paper on top of this one—and the marks had gone through."

"Right!" said McGurk, as triumphant as if *he'd* made the discovery. "So what did Officer Rockaway do? He did what every alert detective should do. Instead of making stupid cracks about Secret Scribblers, he investigated closer. Go on, Joey."

I was blushing a bit now.

8

"Yes. Well. To make the marks of the writing clearer, I very gently shaded over it with a soft-lead pencil. And *this* is what I got."

I turned the scrap over.

Wanda and Willie leaned so close I had to pull the scrap out of the way of their dripping hair. But I'd done a good job with the shading and the words stood out white and clear enough for them to read.

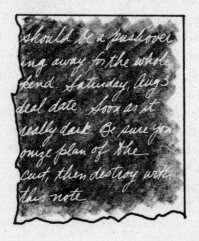

> should be a pushover
> ing away for the whole
> kend. Saturday, Aug 3
> deal date. Soon as it
> really dark. Be sure you
> onize plan of the
> cut, then destroy with
> this note

There was no look of scorn or doubt on Wanda's face now as she said:

"Hey! This about a 'pushover'—it looks like he was writing about a crime."

"That makes it sound like a robbery to me,"

I said. "Especially with that bit about someone going away for the whole weekend."

Willie grunted.

"Where's it say that? I don't see anything about a weekend."

"No?" said Wanda. "But what else could 'kend' be but the end of the word? And look—'ing'—it just has to be the end of 'going.' Right, McGurk?"

Now her eyes were glowing just as enthusiastically as McGurk's.

"Exactly!" he said. Then he hurried on before anyone else could say it. "And 'deal' is the end of 'ideal'—the 'ideal date' for the robbery. And 'orize' is the end of 'memorize'—for 'memorize plan.' " He thumped the table in his glee. "It just has to be a robbery. Timed for Saturday, August 3rd. Three days from now."

Willie was still staring at the note.

"How about 'cuit'?" he said. "What's that mean?"

McGurk shrugged.

"The end of some other word—what else?"

"What other word?"

"How should *I* know, Willie? 'Biscuit,' maybe. Maybe some code word. . . . Anyway, we can't let *that* hold us up. We have enough to be working on with what we *have* deciphered.''

Suddenly Wanda's enthusiasm seemed to leave her. Her shoulders slumped and she began fingering her wet hair.

''Yes,'' she said. ''But so what, McGurk? I agree—it does look like a robbery plan. But *where?* And who's going to do it?''

McGurk glared at her.

''That's the *mystery,* Officer Grieg! That's just what we have to get to work on! Right, Joey?''

This time all my own doubts started drifting back.

''Yes,'' I said. ''But how? Where do we start?''

McGurk rolled his eyes up at the ceiling.

''How? Where? . . . We have the guy's handwriting, don't we? That should narrow it down, shouldn't it? A good handwriting expert should be able to tell us all *kinds* of things about him: how old he is, how big he is, how healthy, how—''

''McGurk!'' Wanda said firmly. *''What* handwriting expert?''

McGurk blinked.

''Why, Brains Bellingham. Who else? He's our crime-lab officer, isn't he? Handwriting

11

analysis is just the kind of thing a guy like Brains should be good at. . . . So I say we all go over to his place now and see what *he* thinks.''

2

Brains Proves His Worth

We were in luck—and I don't mean simply because the rain had slacked off. I mean because Brains was free at last.

The insurance investigator was just leaving when we arrived. We could tell who it was from what he was saying to Mrs. Bellingham in the doorway. We stood politely on one side until he was through.

"Don't worry about a thing, Mrs. Bellingham," he said. (He was tall, with gray wavy hair and a kind smile.) "Now that I've spoken with Gerald, I'm perfectly satisfied." (Gerald is Brains's real name.) "It was a genuine accident. It wasn't even the boy's fault. The warning system he'd fixed up was correct in every detail. It was one of the components that was faulty. Could have happened to anyone."

His smile broadened as he shook Mrs. Bellingham's hand.

"And I have to tell you this," he went on. "For a boy of ten, he sure knows his electronics."

Mrs. Bellingham is a quiet little woman, with dark hair and glasses. Her eyes lit up at this praise for her son, and she blushed.

"He's always been fond of science," she said, smiling shyly around at us, as if hoping we'd support that statement.

That's the way McGurk took it, anyway, for he suddenly chipped in with:

"Yes, *ma'am!*" He turned to the investigator. "Br—uh—Gerald is our crime-lab officer. We're investigators, too."

The man's eyes widened and he looked about to say something—but McGurk seemed to remember the urgency of our own mission.

"May we see him now, Mrs. Bellingham?"

"Sure," she said, stepping aside. "He's up in his room. Go ahead." Then she called out over our heads: "Gerald! You have some more visitors."

Well, I have to say one thing before going any further. An orderly, tidy, scientific mind doesn't have to live in orderly, tidy surroundings. I mean, Brains himself is tidy enough. Don't get me wrong. He's always clean and neatly dressed, and the way he wears his yellow hair—very short and bristly—seems to strengthen this appearance. But his *room*—our *crime lab*—whew!

It was a *mess!*

The table was littered with colored wires and little clocks and switches and batteries and an old radio. All this must have been part of his flood-warning system.

The bed was littered with more wires and switches and things, as well as plans and charts, a battered old microscope, a Polaroid camera, a bunch of test tubes in a rack, and the big black box which he'd once used for his Invisibility Machine.

And there was more.

On the floor, all over, so that you had to be careful where you stepped: piles of science books and science magazines.

On the walls: more charts, tables of figures, graphs, diagrams, blown-up photographs of fingerprints and tire tracks, and what looked like a set of Before and After pictures of a human liver taken from a poison victim. In color.

"Yuk!" said Wanda, turning away so quickly she knocked over a pile of magazines.

"Nice of you all to stop by," said Brains, blinking through his big round glasses and looking very pleased with himself. "I just had a visitor—a real insurance investigator—and he says—"

"We know," said McGurk. "Congratulations! But we're here on business, Officer Bellingham."

"Crime business? Or science business?"

"Both," said McGurk—whereupon all the bristly hairs on Brains's head seemed to stiffen, and he looked very attentive. "It's a clue," McGurk went on. "A clue to a robbery that's going to be pulled off on Saturday. Show him, Joey."

I started to hand Brains the scrap of paper.

16

He shook his head and frowned and said, "Hold it!"

Then he rummaged on the bed and came up with a pair of tweezers. He took the note off me with these, holding it by one corner.

While Brains peered at the skeleton message, McGurk explained how I'd found it and what we'd already decided.

"So what we want to know from *you*, Brains, is this: Can you give us a really accurate description of the guy from this sample of his writing?''

McGurk didn't actually add ''Ho! ho!'' to show that it was a ridiculous question, and that *of course* he knew Brains could do such a simple task in his sleep. But he did wink at the rest of us, and grin.

Then the grin began to fade as Brains's frown began to deepen.

''Well,'' our crime-lab officer said slowly, ''this dumb pencil shading doesn't make it easy. If you'd asked, I could have rigged up an ultra-violet box, like they have in banks and places like that, to look for forgeries and alterations.''

''A what?''

''An ultra-violet box. Where the light inside shows up the faintest markings *without* having to scribble all over them and—''

''I'm sorry!'' I mumbled, suddenly feeling a little foolish, and worried about what McGurk might say next.

But he doesn't believe in raking over old mistakes when he's hot on the scent. It was Brains he was scowling at, not me, as he said:

''So all right! So you're the science expert! But it looks clear enough to me. So get to the handwriting. What does it tell us about the writer? Come on, Brains. You must know something about it. I bet you have a dozen books on the subject right here.''

''Well—sure—one or two. But look—'' Suddenly Brains started acting all businesslike again. ''First, why don't we test whether I am any good at it or not?'' He put the scrap of paper down on the table in a nest of wires and transistors. Then he picked up a scratch pad and began tearing off sheets and handing them out to us. ''Each of you write something down—anything—but don't let me see what you're writing. And don't put your name on it. Then I'll try to identify each one correctly.''

This sounded interesting. So interesting that we even forgot about the Secret Scribbler's note for a while, as we each went into a corner and turned our backs and cupped our hands around the paper and wrote a sample.

And here are those samples—which I kept for our records, and which I'll simply number:

#1. *The quick brown fox jumped over the lazy dog*

#2. (And this one was disguised.)

#3. *I bet you don't guess this!*
Dear Brains, Hi! Sincerely, X

#4. *By hook or by crook I'll be*
last in ~~the~~ this book.

When we were all through, Brains told McGurk to collect the papers and shuffle them. Then he took them and, picking up a pencil, said:

"Just to make it more scientific, I'll write my opinion on the back of each one."

"Why more scientific?" said McGurk, impatiently. "Why not just look and tell us out loud?"

"Because if I did that, I'd be able to tell from your faces whether I was right or not—and that way I'd be sure to get at least the last one or two correct."

He was writing all the time he was speaking, so it didn't really take long. And when he was through he showed us what he had written.

21

On the back of Sample #1:

Orderly, fair-minded, thorough, good at English. Not a genius, but pretty intelligent. Greetings, Joey!

On the back of Sample #2:

Smart, outgoing, eager — and very boastful. Probably has red hair and freckles, from the way he dots his i's and does his loops. How'm I doing, McPeek?

On the back of Sample #3:

Warm heart under a cool exterior. A great tree-climber (see those tall capitals). Hi there, Wanda!

On the back of Sample #4:

Slow to grasp new ideas, but great determination. Probably puts all his effort into developing just one of his five senses. Right, Willie?

We were astonished.

"Gosh!"

"Wow!"

"*Hey*, man!"

"That's pretty good, Brains. You really are a handwriting expert!"

The guy had been one hundred percent correct.

But Brains was shaking his head and smiling.

"Sorry to disappoint you," he said. "But this proves nothing of the kind."

"But—"

"The reason I was able to identify your writing correctly wasn't because of the *way* you wrote. It was *what* you wrote. I mean who but McGurk could write a thing like that? Or Willie this? Or—well—you see what I mean?"

I nodded. McGurk groaned.

"So you're telling us you *can't* give us a description of the guy who wrote this?"

Brains shrugged.

"Well, not exactly. Apart from what *he* wrote. I mean I'd say he was a thief, and fairly well-educated, and—"

"Some crime-lab officer *you* are!" howled McGurk. "*We* could tell that!"

Brains looked unshaken, cool, scientific.

"Then again," he said, "he might be a joker. Or a crime-story writer or something. The note needn't be about a *real* crime."

McGurk turned to the rest of us. His face was twisted with disgust and disappointment.

"Aw, come on, men! We're wasting our

time in this dump. *Some* crime lab! *Some* handwriting expert!"

"No, listen." Brains was still very cool as he held up his hand. "I'm not saying it *is* a joke. I'm just saying it might be. As for being a handwriting expert, let me tell you something. The real ones, the ones the police use in court, they don't mess around with *character* readings. They're scientists, not fortune-tellers. What *they're* expert at is identification. At saying whether a particular sample of writing matches another sample—whether a particular person wrote it or not. O.K.?"

We were quiet now. This seemed to make sense. Even McGurk was beginning to look interested.

"Yeah—well . . ."

"Now if you could find out who *might* have written this," Brains went on, "and you gave me a sample of his writing, I'd probably be able to tell you if he really *did* write this. You know. By careful comparison of . . ."

He trailed off. He sounded as if he was falling asleep, but his eyes had widened instead of closed. He'd been holding the scrap of paper (still by the tweezers) and he'd happened to turn it over.

"Hey! Now this *is* interesting!"

He was staring at the scribble on the back.

"Oh, forget the scribble!" said McGurk. "If you can't tell us anything about the handwriting, what's the use of—?"

"No! This is very important! This makes me pretty sure the writer *wasn't* joking!"

"Eh? Why?"

"Because this 'scribble,' as you call it, is part of a burglar-alarm circuit. Whoever wrote the note sent a plan of the burglar-alarm system along with it. Probably so his accomplice would know just how to put it out of action during the robbery."

We stared at the scribble, and at Brains.

McGurk's eyes were shining now.

It looked as if our new crime-lab officer was proving his worth after all!

3

Wanda Has a Better Idea

"Plan of a burglar-alarm system?" Wanda looked doubtful. "*This* old scribble?"

Brains nodded.

"Yes. Look. This thing like an open drawbridge. That's the sign for a switch. And this. It looks like a corned-beef sandwich to you,

27

maybe—but it's really the power source. And this round thing here's a warning light. And here—where it says SCR—''

"Ah, yes!" said Willie. "We worked that one out, didn't we, McGurk? That stands for Scribbler. The Secret Scribbler.''

Brains made a clicking noise with his tongue. He looked and sounded just like a teacher then.

"Secret Scribbler nothing! That stands for Silicon Controlled Rectifier. They use them in burglar-alarm circuits where a very small signal voltage turns on a very powerful device. Like a bell or a bleeper or something similar. A device that can only be stopped by a complete power shut-off.''

"Wow!" said Willie.

"Sure," said McGurk, trying to look as if he really understood.

"Hey, yes!" I said. "And that solves another little mystery. In the note. The part of a word—'cuit.' It wasn't 'biscuit.' It was 'circuit.' Look!''

I turned the note over, causing Brains to cluck again because I hadn't used the tweezers.

" 'Be sure to memorize plan of *circuit*,' '' I read out, " 'then destroy with this note.' ''

McGurk was nodding fiercely.

"Yeah! So now we have a picture of what

happened. Someone who knew about the circuit draws the plan for his buddy—his accomplice. Then he turns the plan over and writes the note on another piece of paper. But he makes one big mistake.''

''What?'' said Willie, looking a bit awed at this sudden leap of McGurk's—from complete bafflement to complete confidence.

''He rests the note paper on top of the plan he's drawn—not thinking the writing would show through as clear as this.''

''Not thinking anyone would be alert enough to spot it, either,'' I reminded McGurk.

''Yeah. That too. Anyway, his accomplice does what he's told. He tears up the plan after he's memorized it, and the note with it. Maybe he throws them in the trash basket. But when he needs a scrap of paper for a bookmark, he uses the piece with part of the plan on it. Nothing incriminating. Just a bit of stupid scribble to anyone else. I mean, it fooled *us*, didn't it?''

''Some of us,'' said Brains.

But McGurk wasn't listening. He was all set to go on, now. And in that mood he doesn't let anything slow him down.

''So now, men,'' he said, ''we have to plan our next move.''

"Yes," I said. "But what?"

McGurk gave me a scornful look.

"Trace the guy who wrote the note—what else? Like I said earlier."

Now it was Wanda who looked scornful.

"Oh, sure! Through his handwriting, you said. It will tell us all about him, you said. His age, his height, color of hair, social-security number—"

"There *are* other ways of tracing him, Officer Grieg." McGurk looked at her pityingly. "Now that our crime lab's come up with this extra information."

"Like what?" said Wanda, not a bit put down, and still very scornful.

"Well—the type of alarm system. I mean, this has to be an inside job. Whoever wrote the note must have access to the plans of the alarm system. So all we have to do," said McGurk, smiling patiently at Wanda before turning to Brains, "is find out which place in this town uses that type of alarm. Right, Brains?"

Brains wasn't looking half so sure of himself this time.

"Well—yes—but—"

"I mean you *can* find out—from this part here—just what make of alarm it is, can't you?"

"Oh, sure!" But Brains spoke slowly, without much confidence. "Give me another hour or two and I'll probably identify it. I have a whole stack of booklets and things on all kinds of alarms. But, McGurk, even if I do—I mean even *when* I do—we could still have a problem."

"Oh?"

"Yes. I mean, there isn't a central register

at City Hall, you know, saying who uses a particular type of burglar alarm. And—"

McGurk's freckles seemed to spray up and out like sparks from a firecracker, as his frown vanished and a big grin appeared.

"*That's* no problem, Brains! I've made a study of burglar alarms myself. Sort of. Just by keeping my eyes open. And I've noticed that every place that has one, they have this box on the wall outside with the name of the alarm system on it. I guess it's to warn people off. Those that might try to break in if they thought there *wasn't* an alarm."

"Right! Right!" Brains was nodding. "Most of them do, I agree. But what I'm saying is there might be dozens of this type in use. All over town. In stores, lofts, factories, offices, private houses. I mean, McGurk, do you realize—?"

"So what?" said McGurk. "It'll give us something to work on. We'll make a list. We'll—"

"We'll spend the rest of the year on it," said Wanda. "Sure! But the robbery's supposed to take place in three days. Unless, of course, the note meant August 3rd *next* year."

"Listen, you! Who's—"

"Who's got such big ideas he ends up being

totally stupid, McGurk? You! I mean, why do you have to make everything so complicated?"

Wanda was flushed. But the gleam in her eyes now was triumphant, not scornful.

"Eh?" yelped McGurk, who must have noticed that gleam, too, and was wondering what he'd overlooked. "Do *you* know a better way?"

"Yes!" said Wanda. "Why don't we just go along to the library and ask them who borrowed the book before Joey's father?"

McGurk's mouth hung open.

But only for a moment.

And you have to hand it to him. Sure, he likes to get all the good ideas himself. But if someone beats him to it, he never tries to make out that the idea *isn't* a good one. He simply takes over.

"You bet!" he said now. "I was just going to suggest that myself. Come on, men!"

A Brush with Lieutenant Kaspar

We had our story ready for the librarian by the time we got there. And this was *my* idea. I had a feeling that she wouldn't give us the information just like that, for no good reason. And we couldn't explain at this stage of the case what it was really about.

"She wouldn't believe us, for one thing," I said.

So I had the old frayed leather bookmark with me when we went up to the counter. It said on it, in faded gold letters, A GIFT FROM SAN DIEGO, and I wasn't lying when I told Mrs. Shaw that I'd found it in the book on Morocco. I had. It belonged to my father. We just kept that last bit to ourselves.

"We're anxious to get it back to the original owner," I said.

"We think it *could* have belonged to the one who borrowed the book before Mr. Rockaway," said Wanda.

"So if you'll just give us the name and address of that person, we'll see it gets back to him," said McGurk, firmly.

"Very public-spirited, I'm sure," said Mrs. Shaw. She is a stern-looking lady who doesn't care to have kids storming into the adult section—particularly those like McGurk, who can never keep their voices down. "And what makes you think I can do that?"

"Well, ma'am"—McGurk can take a hint; his voice had dropped to almost a whisper, and a sickly grin was squirming its way across his face—"it might be a very valuable keepsake.

Someone might be going half out of their mind right now, not being able to find it.''

Mrs. Shaw didn't seem moved.

"Very touching. But my question was— what makes you think I *can* do that, even if I wished?''

"You keep records of borrowers, don't you, Mrs. Shaw?" said Wanda, who was looking worried now that her idea wasn't working.

"Only for books out on loan. If you knew the title and the book wasn't on the shelves, I *could* give you the name and address of the

37

borrower then. But not after it's been brought back. Anyway, look—why don't you simply let me have that, and I'll put it in a prominent place on the counter. Then when the person comes in and sees it, he or she can claim it.''

I suddenly had a vision of my father coming in and seeing the bookmark there, wondering, and then *asking* how it got there.

"Well," I said, "maybe it isn't worth taking up the space after all.''

"Such a *valuable* keepsake as this? Come now, Joey. Give it to me. Or you'll have your red-haired friend here in tears.''

So we had to leave it there, draped over an empty vase on the counter, for everybody to see.

"And now that we've tried out the really simple idea, the really dumb idea, *your* idea," said McGurk, glaring at Wanda as we went through the lobby, "we'll get back to the intelligent one, the complicated one, *my* idea. Brains, I want you to go all out on identifying that burglar-alarm system and—''

"Well, well, well! If it isn't the boy scientist I was telling you about.''

We'd nearly bumped into two men who were on their way into the library. The speaker was none other than the insurance investigator, and

he had a big smile on his friendly face as he looked down at Brains.

But it was the other face that most of us were looking back up at. A more familiar face. And not very friendly. It had the smallest of smiles under those cold blue eyes.

"Yes," this second man said to the investigator. "Not to mention the boy detective *I* try not to tell *anyone* about!"

It was Lieutenant Kaspar of the police department. He was looking at McGurk, and as he did so his smile got even smaller until it became nothing but a twitch. I guess he was remembering his run-in with McGurk and how we'd solved The Case of the Nervous Newsboy while the police were still floundering.

But McGurk didn't take it like that. If the lieutenant had grinned from ear to ear and hugged McGurk like a long-lost son, that kid couldn't have brightened up faster. Maybe he'd been feeling a bit jealous of all the praise the insurance investigator had been heaping on Brains.

"You bet!" he said to the insurance man. "I'm Jack P. McGurk of the McGurk Organization. Like I told you before, we're investigators too, and Brains here is our crime-lab expert. I *discovered* him."

"You don't say!" said the smiling insurance man.

"We're very busy," said Kaspar, really scowling now. "Just move aside. You're standing in our way."

But McGurk didn't seem to hear him.

"In fact, we're working on an interesting case right now, Lieutenant. We've had word that a big robbery's going down on Saturday, and—"

"Oh?" Lieutenant Kaspar looked a little more alert. "Word? What word? Who from?"

"Well, really it was a clue. Just a scrap of paper. We found it in a library book. Show him, Joey."

But Kaspar seemed to have lost interest. He took one look at the scrap of paper with its scribble on one side and the mess of black shading on the other, and he turned pink.

"Look!" he said. "Go play your games yourselves. We're busy. Much too busy to waste time on some childish Join-the-Dots Puzzle. . . . This way, John."

"But, *sir!*" McGurk had sidestepped into his path. "This is serious!"

The lieutenant's face got a shade pinker. Even the insurance investigator was looking annoyed, but at least he started to explain that they had come to check out the security arrangements at the library, where there was going to be a special art exhibition in the fall, with some very valuable pictures on loan. I mean, you couldn't *really* blame the men for getting sore.

But the lieutenant had had enough.

"Listen!" he said, stabbing a finger at McGurk's chest. "As head of a detective organization *surely* you know there are other crimes besides robbery. Right?"

"Y-yes. Sure!"

"Then you might be aware there is such a crime as Obstructing a Police Officer in the Course of His Duties."

"But—"

"Which is what you are doing right now, sonny! So do you get out of my way—*all* of you—or do I have to book you?"

We'd melted even before he'd finished. And McGurk wasn't the *last* to move.

But he was mad himself now. It was as if he'd decided that bright pink was the correct color for all angry police chiefs—because that was exactly the shade his own face had gotten.

"All right!" he muttered, as we went through the doorway. "You heard him. You were all witnesses. You saw how I tried to report the planning of a genuine crime to him, and how he wouldn't listen. Well, that gives us a clear field, men. It's up to the McGurk Organization to see this thing through alone now!"

He spoke as if he'd meant to report the matter to the police all along, the way a good citizen should. I mean, he was so indignant that anyone would have thought that he'd actually gone to police headquarters to inform Lieutenant Kaspar, instead of just meeting the man by accident and blabbering it all out boastfully.

But no one pointed this out to McGurk. Not

even Wanda. We were all feeling pretty sore ourselves. One of us especially.

"Don't worry, McGurk," said Brains. "I'll go straight home and work on the alarm-system angle." His face was pale, his eyes were rolling angrily, and his hair looked more bristly than ever. "Any adult who mistakes an electronic circuit for a Join-the-Dots Puzzle *deserves* to be shown up for the dummy he is!"

RK ORGANIZATION

5

Willie Makes a Discovery

Well, it didn't take Brains long to identify that
system. He had the answer for us right after
lunch, when we met in McGurk's basement.

"It's a product of the Ace-Sentinel Alarm
Company," he said. "No doubt about it."

"Great!" cried McGurk, jumping to his
feet. "So now all we have to do is go around

town looking for the Ace-Sentinel sign on the walls. . . . No?''

Brains was shaking his head.

''That's the trouble,'' he said. ''It's one of the most popular systems there are. I mean, Wanda was right. The list will be so long, it'll take us the rest of the year to check it out.''

McGurk looked outraged. Then hurt. Then beseeching.

''But—you're *sure?* You're sure it couldn't be part of the plan for some other system? Some very *rare* system? With only one or two in use in the whole town?''

Brains's top lip curled slightly.

''Listen,'' he said. ''I'm a scientist. A crime-lab scientist. And a crime-lab scientist has to report on what's *true,* not what's *easy.* I'm sorry, McGurk, but there's no mistaking it.'' He tossed the scrap of paper onto the table. He wasn't fooling around with tweezers this time. ''That's part of the Ace-Sentinel Company's best-selling SCR system.''

The scrap had fluttered across to where Willie was sitting. And as McGurk groaned over Brains's report, Willie picked up the paper and glared at it. I guess he wanted to show how disgusted he was with it, too.

''Look,'' I said anxiously. ''Be careful how

you handle it, Willie. It's still part of the record and—"

"Hey! You catch a *whiff* of something on it, Willie?"

McGurk spoke respectfully as well as hopefully. He has great faith in Willie's sense of smell.

But this time—as if to pay Brains back for what he'd written about Willie's handwriting, to show the crime-lab expert he didn't know *everything*—Willie was using one of his other senses.

Sure, he was holding that scrap of paper pretty close to his nose. But he was also holding it up to the light and peering at it.

Or *through* it.

"No," he murmured. "It doesn't smell much of anything. Except lead pencils, maybe."

"So put it down then!" snapped McGurk. "And give it to Joey. It's an important piece of evidence."

Willie continued to peer up at—or through—the scrap.

"I know that," he murmured. Then suddenly his eyes widened and his voice rose to a kind of bleat. "But *hey! Yeah!* I'm sure of it! This *is* a piece of Chainmail Wove!"

"Eh?"

We looked at one another. Had Willie gone crazy with all this concentrated detective work?

"Chainmail Wove!" said Willie, very confident now. "It's a new line of my father's. He sells paper, you know, and he's talked about nothing else for weeks."

McGurk was gaping at him. Then he gulped.

"Sure, sure, Willie! But—how can you tell?"

"From the watermark. See for yourself."

At the word "watermark," Brains stiffened up.

"Good idea, Willie! Here—let me help."

Then he took the scrap from Willie and held it closer to the lamp above the table, at a better angle, so that we could all see the pattern clearly.

Here's a rough sketch of it, magnified:

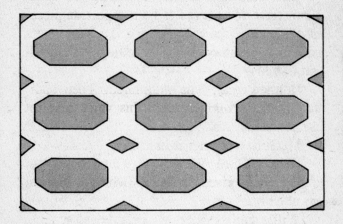

Like that—a kind of white chain pattern—all over the paper.

"I should have thought of this myself," said Brains. "Very good identification—watermarks. I have a book with over three hundred examples."

"Well, you won't find this one in it!" said Willie, proudly. "Like I said, it's a brand-new product. My father only started selling it last month. In fact, it's been a big headache for him."

"Why?" I asked.

"Never mind that!" said McGurk. "We've got problems of our own."

But Willie was already answering my question. And that proved to be a good thing.

"Because it's so expensive. Dad says he's worried because it's not selling very well around here."

I turned to McGurk.

"So that's *another* way of tracing the Secret Scribbler!"

McGurk was onto it in a flash.

"Hey! Sure! Willie—do you think your father could give us a list of who he's sold it to already?"

Willie smiled sadly. My heart began to sink. "Here it comes," I thought. "Another needle-in-the-haystack job!"

But Willie's sadness was for his father's problem, not ours.

"Here?" he said. "In this town? Easy!" he said, sighing heavily. "Just one place. An office-supply firm downtown."

"An office-supply firm?" said Wanda. "But doesn't that mean they resell it in smaller quantities to other people?"

"Yes," said Willie. "Only according to my father they've been grumbling—saying they wished they hadn't bought such a big supply from him.''

"So that means *they* can't have sold it to many places yet!" said McGurk. "Hey! Do you think your father could get a list from *them?* Of people they've supplied? It can't be such a long one, and—''

McGurk's hopes were raised so high he couldn't trust himself to say any more. He just looked pleadingly at Willie, with fingers crossed on both hands.

He wasn't the only one to freeze with suspense.

We all stared at Willie—until he started blushing as if he'd done something wrong.

Then he shrugged and smiled uneasily.

"Maybe," he said. "I'll ask him when he comes home tonight—O.K.?"

"You do that, Officer Sandowsky," said McGurk, making it an official order. "And you go along with him, Officer Rockaway, just to make sure he asks nice and tactfully. We can't afford to blow this one. It's the best lead we've got now. The whole case depends on it!"

Willie's Father Makes a Promise

Willie's father didn't need any tactful handling. Mr. Sandowsky was a pleasure to do business with. In fact, Mr. Sandowsky is a shining example of how *all* adults ought to act when dealing with kids who have important problems on their minds.

He didn't brush us off.

He didn't put us down.

He didn't kid around.

When Willie and I went up to him as he was getting out of his car, and Willie said, "Hey, Dad! We need your help!" Mr. Sandowsky didn't scowl and say, "All right, all right! So let me get in the house first!" or, "Why? What have you broken *this* time?"

No.

He just loosened his necktie, and put down his briefcase, and sat down on the front doorstep, and said:

"O.K. Tell me about it."

He is a big man, very tall. Otherwise he doesn't look a bit like Willie. He has a very short stubby nose and his hair is blond.

"It's about that new writing paper, Dad. That Chainmail Wove."

This time a frown did cross Mr. Sandowsky's face. But it was a gentle one, more sad than mad.

"Oh, *that!*" he said. "Well, fellas, if it's free samples you want for your detective club, I'm sorry. It's too expensive. I could let you have some other—"

"No, no, Mr. Sandowsky!" I said. "It's

nothing like that. But it does have something to do with detective work.''

"Oh?''

Mr. Sandowsky looked genuinely interested.

"Yes, Dad! It's about watermarks. We—we—''

Willie dried up. We had decided not to tell Mr. Sandowsky *exactly* why we needed his help, at this stage. But talking around a thing delicately and carefully isn't Willie's bag. Which is why McGurk had been right to send me along too.

I took over.

"It's like this, Mr. Sandowsky. If a detective finds a clue and it's a scrap of paper and he wants to know who wrote on it''—I took a deep breath—"can he trace the writer from the watermark?''

Mr. Sandowsky looked more interested than ever.

"Well—maybe not directly. Especially if it was a popular brand. But—''

"But if it was a *new* brand, Dad? Like Chainmail Wove?''

Mr. Sandowsky sighed and loosened his necktie some more. Then he grinned.

"Well, that's another ball game altogether.

Sure. Yes. If the scrap was Chainmail Wove, in *this* town, you'd have narrowed the list of suspects down considerably—I'm sorry to say!"

"Oh, boy!" I cried. Then: "Gee, I'm sorry, Mr. Sandowsky. I was thinking of it from the detective angle. But you mean you could say, right now, just who had a stock of this paper?"

"Sure could! The Betta Office Supply Company. Two hundred reams of the stuff."

"But would we—would a detective be able to find out who'd bought it in smaller quantities from *them?*"

"Unfortunately, yes! The manager of Betta Office Supplies was beefing about it just today. Saying how he'd sold only three half-reams this past month."

I caught my breath.

Willie had even closed his eyes.

"Did—did he say who'd bought them?" I managed to stammer.

"No. But come to think of it, I might just ask him that myself. It would be interesting to know exactly what kind of people are prepared to pay so much extra for that quality paper. Hey!" He laughed and clapped a hand on my shoulder. "Thanks for giving me the idea! It'll be something to put in my monthly report to Head Office.''

"You're welcome, sir," I said. "Uh—will you be letting Willie know just how many names are on the list? And who they are?''

"Sure! Why not? It'll give you all something to do if it rains again. You can make believe that a clue with a Chainmail Wove watermark on it really has turned up. Then you can spend the rest of the week in that basement of Jack McGurk's arguing about which place it came from!'' He got up, still smiling, pleased to have been helpful. "See you around Joey. . . .''

And that's what I mean about Mr. Carl W.

Sandowsky being a real true gentleman and a sport and a shining example to all adults.

In fact, ten minutes later, after we'd told McGurk of Mr. Sandowsky's cooperation and promise, the Head of the Organization said, solemnly and sincerely:

"Willie—if we ever allowed adults to join the Organization and be issued an ID card, your father would be first in line."

But his fingers were crossed when he said it, and I know why.

Mr. Sandowsky's promise was sincere. His spirit of cooperation couldn't be doubted. But the big question remained:

Would he be able to deliver?

7

The List

We had to wait the whole of the next day before we found out the answer to that question.

During that time, we tried to be content with getting on with the alarm-system inquiry. And *that* was just as we'd figured: a dog of a job. There were Ace-Sentinel signs everywhere. On the walls of stores, factories, offices, private houses. It made me marvel why I'd never noticed them before: bright red boxes with ACE-SENTINEL ALARMS written in yellow letters, and a bolt of yellow lightning striking across them. I even began to see them whenever I closed my eyes.

"And we still haven't covered half of the town!" said Wanda, late in the afternoon.

We were waiting around on my front lawn, which is next to Willie's.

"Yes," said Brains, looking up from the bunch of lists we'd made. "And not all places display the sign, you know. There may be dozens we've missed already."

"Let's hope that Willie's father doesn't let us down," I said.

"You sure this is the time he usually gets home, Willie?" McGurk asked.

He was frowning so much that his freckles were all bunched up in a brown blur around his eyes—a sure sign that he was getting worried.

Willie was the only one to look cheerful.

"Sure! He's—" Then his eyes widened. "Uh-uh! Here he comes now." All at once even Willie began to look nervous. "Keep your fingers crossed, guys!" he murmured, going over into his own driveway.

We watched as Willie waited at the side of the car. We saw Mr. Sandowsky get out and we all held our breath. We kept holding it, as we watched Willie look up and open his mouth and say something. And when Mr. Sandowsky quickly shook his head, that breath of ours came out in three sad sighs and one deep groan. The groan was McGurk's.

But wait a minute!

Willie wasn't sighing or groaning. Willie was grinning all over his face. And when he held out his hand, and Mr. Sandowsky lifted his knee to balance his briefcase, and opened the lid, and pulled out a piece of paper, and gave it to Willie—we cheered. We just couldn't help ourselves.

Then Willie came skipping and dancing across into my front yard like he'd just won the million-dollar lottery, crying: "He did it! He got it! It's here!"

"What did your father shake his head for?" I asked him, before he'd reached us.

"Eh? Oh—that! That was when I asked him did he have any trouble getting the list and he said—"

"Willie!" growled McGurk. "The list! Give!"

"Oh—yeah—sure!"

Then Willie handed it over to McGurk and we all crowded around and read the neatly typed list of names and addresses.

It didn't take long.

There had only been three customers for Chainmail Wove paper.

They were:

MORELLI'S FLOWER SHOP
163 ELM STREET

JUNIPER SHADES FUNERAL HOME
235 WILSON BOULEVARD

R. J. MENDOZA
72 MAIN STREET

"Elm Street," said Brains, glancing through our own much bigger lists. "We were there

this afternoon, but I don't remember an alarm
sign outside the flower store.''

"Well, why should there be?" said Wanda.
"Someone might go in during the day to hold
them up for the money in the cash register. But
who'd break in over the weekend to steal *flow-
ers?''*

"Yes," I said. "And the same goes for the
second on the list. Who'd want to burglarize
a funeral home? And don't forget this. It's an
inside job. Whoever wrote the note had access
to that paper. So"—I grinned at the thought—
"unless you're figuring it was one of the
corpses that came to life in the middle of the

night, and reached out from the casket for a pen and—"

"Not so fast!" said McGurk, with a strange gleam in his eyes. "Hey! Wow! What if the Secret Scribbler is one of the mortician's assistants and he's planning a *corpse* robbery?"

"Oh, come on, McGurk!" said Wanda. "You've been seeing too many horror movies!"

"You—you mean like grave robbers, McGurk?" said Willie, a strange gleam coming into his eyes, too.

Even Brains seemed impressed with this one.

"It *could* be, I guess," he said. "Some scientist, needing fresh bodies to experiment with."

I groaned.

These guys *wanted* it to be the funeral home!

"Well, it isn't down on our list," I said. "And I covered Wilson Boulevard personally. *But*"—I went on, before Brains could point out once again that not everyone who had an alarm system displayed the sign—"this R. J. Mendoza *is*. Look. You wrote it down yourself, McGurk."

With a last wistful glance at the funeral home on the list, McGurk turned to where I was pointing.

"Yeah," he grunted. "So I did. Only I can't remember what kind of place it was now."

"Well, I *can!*" said Wanda, suddenly brightening up. "Because I even bought something there myself once. It's a *jewelry* store!"

McGurk's face got pale. Every freckle stood out sharply and his eyes seemed to be lit up from behind.

"A *jewelry* store? You're *sure?*"

Wanda nodded rapidly, flushed with excitement.

"Positive!"

Then McGurk slapped Willie's father's list triumphantly. It was easy to see that he'd forgotten all about corpses and grave robbers.

"So that must be it!" he said. "A jewel heist! Of course! What else?" He glared around. "So what are we waiting for, men? Let's get with it!"

8
The Sample

Well, we didn't know it at that moment, but what we *were* waiting for was the store to open next day.

When we got down to Main Street that afternoon—running all the way—it was 5:37, and the gate was up across the doorway of Number 72, and the grill was over the window.

But maybe it was just as well. If we'd been able to go straight in there, without a proper plan, we might have blown everything. Some of us, for instance, wanted to warn the owner right away.

"Let's see if we can get him on the phone," I said.

"Or bang on the gate," said Willie. "Maybe he lives up there, over the store."

"Yes," said Wanda. "He ought to be alerted as soon as possible."

"Hold it!" said McGurk, who was only just getting his breath back. (He'd been wasting more than anyone else, yelling at us to hurry, all the way there.) "What's—what's the rush? The note said Saturday. It's only Thursday."

"But why delay it any longer?" I asked.

"Why? Because this is an *inside* job, Officer Rockaway. Whoever wrote that note must work here. One of the clerks. And I'd like to go in when they're open and check them out before we make our final move."

"It doesn't have to be a clerk," I said, feeling a bit miffed. "It could have been the electrician who installed the alarm. Right, Brains?"

But Brains was on McGurk's side again.

"I doubt it. Those guys are picked especially for their honesty. And why would he also know Mr. Mendoza's movements? Like exactly when the owner's going away for the weekend?"

Willie was still staring at McGurk.

"What do you mean, check them out, McGurk?"

"Well—narrow them down. Suppose there's a man and woman clerk and Brains here could tell us whether a male or female wrote the note. Then we'd know which one it was, wouldn't we?"

But this time Brains wasn't going along with him.

"Sorry, McGurk. I told you before. The only *scientific* way I can help is to match an actual sample with the note. We need to get specimens of *both* clerks' handwriting and check them against the note before we can be sure."

"Just a minute!" said Wanda. "What makes you all think there's more than one clerk, a small store like this? There was only one when I bought my mother a scarf pin here last Christmas. A girl."

"So that makes it easier!" said McGurk, all smiles again. "First thing tomorrow, as soon

as they're open, we'll come back here and get a sample of her handwriting.''

"Oh, yes? Just like that? How?''

"Nothing to it! We just buy something and get her to write out a sales slip!''

And so, the following morning, looking very tense, we all trooped into the jewelry store. It hadn't been easy, deciding what to buy, when the Organization's petty-cash fund had in it only two dollars and thirty-seven cents. In fact we still weren't sure whether the store would have anything for as little as that.

When we closed the door behind us, a girl looked up from some trays of rings she was arranging under the glass-topped counter. She wasn't very old—maybe seventeen—and she had a pleasant smiling face under a lot of dark hair. I remember thinking at the time how dumb it was to go by people's looks—especially when the owner of the store shot his head out around a door in the back, to see who'd walked in. Now *he* did look like a villain. He had bushy black eyebrows and a big oily grin on his face—until he saw it was just a bunch of kids. Then he scowled and said:

"You handle these, Carol. And see they don't fool around.''

"Yes, Mr. Mendoza," said the girl, with a sigh and a roll of the eyes for him and a quick wink and another smile for us. "Can I help you?" she asked politely.

"Yes, please," said McGurk. "I'd like a new watchband."

"Sure," said the girl. She reached for a tray from a shelf at the back. "How about one of these expanding bracelets? There's this gold-plated one. It runs one hundred and fifteen dollars. Or maybe this one in stainless steel—twenty-seven fifty. . . . No?"

McGurk's face was scarlet. He was shaking his head.

"I was thinking of something cheaper," he said. "It isn't a gift. It's only for me."

"Ah, yes, of course." The girl still smiled as sweetly as when she'd expected McGurk to be interested in the gold bracelet. "Well, how about one of these leather ones? Only ten dollars and that includes—no?"

"I—look, miss—don't you have anything under *three* dollars?"

The girl's smile *still* remained—warm and friendly and kind.

"Well, yes," she said. "Of course. How stupid of me! There're a few of these canvas ones left. They mightn't look like much, but they're nice bright colors and very strong. Best of all, they're only a dollar ninety-five without tax.''

"I'll take that one," said McGurk, pointing quickly, without fussing about the colors.

"You want me to fix it for you?"

"No, thanks. I'll just take it with me."

This should have been our big moment—when the girl had worked out the tax and McGurk had handed over the money.

But two things spoiled it.

First, we weren't all that keen to get the girl into trouble now, after all. At least I wasn't, and I think some of the others felt the same way.

And the second thing was when she put the money in the cash register and turned a handle and gave McGurk a little printed slip with his purchase.

"Thank you," she said. "Have a good day."

"Hey—but!"

McGurk was staring down at the slip as if it had bitten his fingers.

"Something wrong?"

"Don't I get a receipt?"

"That's it," said the girl. "See. One ninety-five plus sixteen cents tax—two dollars eleven cents. And there's the date, August 2nd. It's all there.''

"No, it isn't! I mean—I'm sorry—but I have to have a *written* receipt. With my name on it and a description of what I bought. I—I need it for our accounts!''

The girl's smile had vanished, but she still looked friendly. And another thing in her favor was that she didn't make any snide cracks about kids having to keep accounts.

But she groaned and said softly:

"You *sure* this printed slip won't do?''

"Positive!''

"O.K.,'' she sighed. "Only I'm not allowed to write receipts since I made a dumb mistake over a receipt for a diamond ring last month.'' She turned her head. "Mr. Mendoza!'' she called out.

We looked at one another in dismay.

We weren't even bothered at the snarly way the owner treated the request—huffing and puffing and grunting as he scribbled out the receipt. When he thrust it at McGurk, muttering, "All for two lousy dollars!'' before going back through the door, we were still too worried about what to do next to take any notice of him and his rudeness.

"See what I mean?'' said the girl, as the

door to the back room slammed shut. "All *I'm* allowed to write is my autograph!"

We nodded and slowly, dejectedly, made for the door.

Then suddenly McGurk stopped and turned, his face all bright again.

"Hey!" he said. "*Would* you? Would you sign your autograph, miss? Please! For my album? I don't have it with me but—" He flicked his fingers. "Joey! Your notebook. . . . If you write it in this," he said, handing it to the girl, "I can cut it out and stick it in my album."

The girl's face brightened too. With a quick defiant glance at the door behind her, she said:

"Sure! Why not? And—hey—you know what? I think I know just the thing to write!"

Well—here it is. The sample we'd come so close to losing:

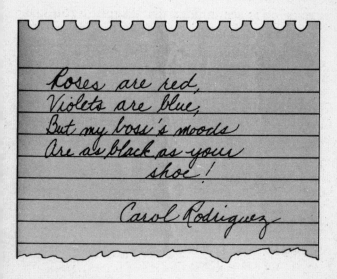

Roses are red,
Violets are blue;
But my boss's moods
Are as black as your
shoe!

Carol Rodriguez

"I like her spirit, anyway!" said Wanda, when we were out on the sidewalk. "That man's a—a real pig!"

McGurk was gloating over the sample.

"Sure! But there you have the motive. She'd do anything to get even with that jerk."

Brains coughed politely.

"Excuse me, McGurk," he said, pointing to the autographed page. "But aren't you going a bit too fast? I've only had a glance at it, but it looks nothing like the writing on the note."

"But that must have been *disguised!*" said McGurk, with a yelp in his voice. "And it's your job to see through that disguise. You said it yourself. Don't tell me—"

"Sure! Sure! I'll be able to check it out all right. But let's get it back to the crime lab and put it under the microscope before we make up our minds!"

McGurk Nearly
Throws It All Away

"I'm sorry!" said Brains Bellingham, for what must have been the fifth time. "But the person who wrote the note is definitely not the one who wrote this autograph."

He looked up from the two specimens on the table in front of him. He had swept a clear space there to make room for his microscope, three different-sized magnifying glasses, and a pile of books on handwriting. He had spent about thirty minutes, bending over the specimens, peering at them, and flipping through his books. He had invited us each in turn to check his observations and personally I had to agree with him. So did Wanda and Willie.

Only McGurk hung on to his hopes to the bitter end.

"But I keep telling you, she must have disguised her handwriting when—"

"And I keep telling *you* that it doesn't show a single one of the Ten Characteristics of Disguised Handwriting!" said Brains firmly.

This was the title of one of his books. It was only a thin pamphlet really, but it had been written by a Scotland Yard expert. Brains had made us go through it with him—point by point. And again I had to agree. I mean, who wants to argue with a Scotland Yard expert?

Even McGurk was forced to shake his head in the end, when Brains offered to take him through the Ten Points one more time.

"All right, all right!" he said, sitting down heavily on Brains's already overloaded bed and

causing the rack of test tubes to rattle. "So it wasn't her."

"It could have been a boyfriend, maybe," said Brains, helpfully. "I mean, it doesn't rule her out entirely."

But McGurk likes his hopes to be fulfilled in a big, bright, clear-cut way. If they aren't, he tends to get depressed.

"Yeah, sure!" he grunted. "But—oh, what's the use? It's Friday already and—and we've wasted nearly three dollars on *this!*"

With his shoulders hunched up dejectedly, he'd plunged his hands into his pants pockets. Now he pulled out the new watchband and looked ready to throw it out of the window.

"Oh, come on, McGurk!" said Wanda. "Nearly *three* dollars? It only cost one ninety-five and—"

"With tax it did! Here! See for yourself!"

McGurk tossed the crumpled receipt at Wanda.

"This is too childish for words!" said Wanda, letting it fall between the heaps of books and magazines at her feet.

"Hey! Don't litter the place up!" said Brains. "My mother's always complaining about it and I only cleaned up this morning."

He could have fooled me. And I must say

I had to smile as I watched Brains stoop so anxiously to pick up that one tiny scrap.

Then my smile froze when I saw the look on his face as he straightened up.

"Hey! Just a minute!" he said, staring at the receipt and suddenly beginning to smooth it out. "Hey! Now *this*—yeah!"

Brushing the girl's autograph to one side, he very carefully laid the receipt alongside the original note.

"What? *What?*"

The test tubes rattled again as McGurk bounded off that bed and knocked over a pile of *New Scientist* magazines on his way to the table.

This time there was no protest from Brains. His eyes were too busy studying the receipt to notice any further mess in the room.

"*This* is the same handwriting as the note. Exactly the same. There hasn't even been an attempt to disguise it. Look. Look at those *t*'s and *s*'s. And the loops. . . ."

And so we looked, and compared, and gasped.

For there was no doubt about it. We didn't need a microscope or a magnifying glass or an expert's textbook this time.

And here's what we saw:

Received from _J. P. McGurk_ _____ _8/2_ 19___

The sum of _Two dollars eleven cents_

for watch band (canvas)

$ _2.11_ _____ _R. J. Mendoza_

R. J. Mendoza was the Secret Scribbler!

"But—I don't understand it!" said McGurk, in a croaky voice. "It—it's all *wrong!*"

"Yeah," said Willie. "He should've filled out the year part. A receipt isn't any good without the full date. My father—"

"Not *that,* you dummy!" cried McGurk. "I mean it's all wrong that he should want someone to knock over his own store!"

But I was way ahead of them all, this time.

"Is it?" I said.

"Well, *sure!* A guy just doesn't go around inviting people to rob him, does he? Unless he's a nut case. Is that what you're thinking?"

"No," I said. "What I am thinking of is the first time we came into this room the other day.

And of who it was who'd just been talking to Brains.''

"Hey!" Now Brains himself had caught up. "Sure! You mean the insurance, right?"

"Right!" I said. "Mendoza has set up this

robbery so he can collect from the insurance company. So he'll not only get the money from *them*, but he'll still have the stuff that was supposed to have been stolen. Then he'll sell it and split whatever he gets for it with the guy who's helping him.''

McGurk's face was glowing now. He was nodding, nodding at everything I was saying.

''That's it!'' he said. ''That just has to be it! And it figures. I mean, I could tell that guy was a crook the minute I set eyes on him.''

''Yes,'' said Wanda. ''And I could tell that Carol *wasn't!*''

''So what do we do next?'' I said. ''Go to the police?''

10

Back to Square One?

Somehow McGurk had managed to find a path between the piles of books and magazines where he could pace up and down. But my question stopped him dead.

"Police? You kidding? Kaspar *still* wouldn't listen."

"He will if we wait until Sunday," said Wanda. "After the robbery's been reported already."

Willie grinned.

"Yeah! And then that old lieutenant is gonna feel pretty stupid!"

But McGurk was shaking his head fiercely.

"What? And let those crooks get away with it? Even for a few hours? Don't you know it's the first duty of an officer to *prevent* crime?"

Willie hung his head, but *I* wasn't fooled. What was really bugging McGurk was the thought of having to wait around, doing nothing.

Which made him all the more eager when Brains said:

"I know what *would* make Lieutenant Kaspar listen to us."

"What?"

"If we could find out who *received* the note. The accomplice."

"Why?"

"Because it's probably someone with a record. I mean, you don't just ask *anyone* to come in and fake a burglary. Especially since the guy's supposed to know something about alarm systems and how to put them out of action."

McGurk still didn't quite get it. With bunched-up freckles, he began:

"But why would the police—?"

"Because," said Brains, "if it's someone with a record—someone they know—then it would *mean* something to them. Then they *would* want to know more."

Wanda's face brightened.

"So that means we're back to Square One," she said. "To that simple idea again. That dumb idea. *My* idea."

"Aw, not the library again!" groaned McGurk.

"Sure, the library!" said Wanda. "Remember what Mrs. Shaw said? There was no way to trace borrowers of books already returned. But if this guy's so interested in Morocco—maybe that's where he's planning to go with his share of the loot—well, then! He might have taken out another book on the subject. And if he's still got it out, then the librarian *can* tell us who."

McGurk's mouth had fallen open.

"It makes sense, McGurk," I said. "After all, there can't be that many books on Morocco—on or off the shelves. My father was grumbling about it only the other day."

But McGurk didn't need any convincing. I

guess he'd just been wondering how to make Wanda's idea his own again. In the end, he decided to go halves with her.

"Officer Grieg," he said, "I knew that library idea of ours wasn't as dumb as it looked. Come on, let's go there now!"

The old leather bookmark was still on the counter, dangling from the mouth of the vase like the tongue of a thirsty dog. But this time

we were luckier. Instead of Mrs. Shaw, it was
Mrs. Grunwald on duty. And she is younger
and smiles more, and is much more friendly to
kids. That made it real easy for McGurk.

"Hi, Mrs. Grunwald!" he said. "I think
we've solved your mystery."

He pointed to the bookmark.

Mrs. Grunwald laughed.

"You and your mysteries, Jack McGurk!"
she said. "All right—what makes you think
you've got the answer to the missing heirloom
here?"

We breathed easier. She obviously knew all
about it. And she was obviously in a very co-
operative mood, even for her.

"Wanda," said McGurk, "explain our rea-
soning, please."

So Wanda told Mrs. Grunwald just what
she'd told us, and even before Officer Grieg
was through, the librarian was leading the way
to the foreign countries stack.

"O.K.," she said, "here we are. Morocco.
And there are just three—no, four—titles on
the shelf here. You want to write them down,
Joey?"

I already had my notebook and pencil out,
and was scribbling away.

"Good!" said Mrs. Grunwald, when I'd fin-

ished jotting the fourth title down. "Now the next thing we have to do is consult the catalog."

Then she led the way to the catalog drawers, pulled one out, and began flipping through the cards.

"There you go," she said, sticking a pencil in to mark the place. "Books on Morocco. Right? So what you do next is go through the cards and see which titles *aren't* on the list you've just made and—bingo!—those are the books out on loan.''

Then she returned to the counter.

Well, there were just four more titles besides the four we'd already seen on the shelves, and one of these extra four was *Touring Morocco with an Open Mind*—which was the book my father had out.

"So that leaves these three," I said.

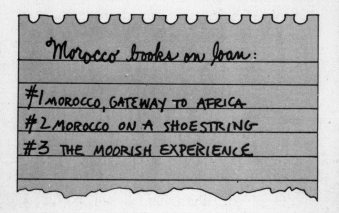

Morocco books on loan:

#1 MOROCCO, GATEWAY TO AFRICA
#2 MOROCCO ON A SHOESTRING
#3 THE MOORISH EXPERIENCE

"And now let's hope Mrs. Grunwald will give us the names of the borrowers," said Wanda, glancing over to the counter.

"Sure she will!" said McGurk. "She's on

our side. Next to Willie's father there isn't another adult I'd rather have in the Organization.''

He was right, too. Mrs. Grunwald didn't even hesitate. As soon as I showed her my list she nodded and got busy on her records behind the counter.

And inside five minutes she had the answers.

"Morocco, Gateway to Africa—that's on loan to Mr. Plimpton, the Principal of the High School. *Morocco on a Shoestring* is out to a Mr. Terence Burch, who I'm afraid I don't know. And *The Moorish Experience* is on long summer loan to Doctor Spencer. He's taken the book with him on vacation to North Africa, in fact. He won't be home until Labor Day.''

We didn't even have to ask for the addresses. She wrote them down on a scrap of paper and wished us luck. Better yet, she called us back as we began to hurry out and said:

"Here! Why don't you take this bookmark with you? Then if you find it belongs to either of the first two you can get it back to him right away.''

I could have kissed her.

"Gee, thanks, Mrs. Grunwald!'' I said. "And don't worry. We'll make sure the original owner gets it.''

Outside, in the lobby, the others were already coming to a decision.

"Well, it isn't likely to be Mr. Plimpton who's helping to fake a jewel heist," said McGurk. "And it certainly can't be Doctor Spencer, because he's out of the country. So that leaves this Burch guy."

"Yes," said Wanda, looking very serious all at once. "And that *does* make sense."

"Oh? You know him?"

"Slightly. He lives on our street. He's about twenty, and I've heard my brother Ed talking about him."

"*Does* he have a record?"

Wanda's frown deepened.

"Well, no . . ." she said slowly. "But there have been rumors. Like how he's not fussy about where he gets his money. And I believe the police once went around to his house to ask about a stolen car."

"Well, then!" McGurk's face was all aglow. "What are we waiting for? We've only to mention his name in connection with the robbery and Lieutenant Kaspar will change his mind just like that. . . . What's wrong *now?*"

Wanda had been chewing her lip.

"Well . . . gee . . . nothing. But—I mean —I did say there'd only been *rumors,* Mc-

Gurk. And—well—it just doesn't seem *fair*. He may get hassled for nothing—and all because of me!"

"Fair?" howled McGurk. "Not *fair?* Look, Officer Grieg, it's practically one hundred percent certain he's in on this, and—"

"Hold it, McGurk!" Brains had a blue gleam in his eyes that was almost as bright as some of McGurk's best green gleams. "I agree with Wanda. But I also agree with you."

"So?"

"So why don't we run one last check? After all, it's only Friday. There's still another thirty-six hours before anything's due to happen. Let's see if we can't get some additional evidence linking the Mendoza store to this guy Burch."

"Yes," I said, seeing the sense of this. "After all, McGurk, it's what we'd have to do if we were real cops—before we could take the case to the D.A."

That did it.

"O.K.," he said. "Fine!" Then he turned to Brains. "But how? Do you have an idea?"

"Do I have an idea!" Brains laughed. "You bet! A real top-grade scientific idea, too. Come closer," he said, lowering his voice, "and I'll outline it for you."

Then the library staff and borrowers who happened to look into the lobby must have seen a very strange sight. Five kids in a tight murmuring huddle that lasted for about two minutes. Then suddenly—like when a cloud breaks to let through the rays of the sun—McGurk's bright red face and flaming hair appeared.

"Oh, boy!" he yelled. "What are we waiting for?"

"Out!" came another yell. "This very minute!"

It was Mrs. Shaw, just back from her lunch break.

But we were already on our way.

11

Brains Takes Some Pictures

At first it looked as if we'd run out of luck.

It was not until late afternoon that we saw Terry Burch. When we did, he wasn't on foot but driving home in a red Mustang, which made it almost impossible for us to carry out Brains's plan.

But then our luck changed.

Just when we were wondering what to do about it, the suspect came out and started cutting his front lawn. And that was perfect, because the first part of the plan was this:

Brains had brought along his Polaroid camera and he wanted to get a good clear shot of Terry Burch without him knowing it.

So now, while the suspect worked away on his lawn—stopping every now and then to turn, or to clear the blades—Brains began to take pictures of us on the sidewalk. Us in all sorts of poses and groups. Like: McGurk in the middle, looking very pompous, with folded arms; McGurk pretending to arrest Willie by putting an armlock on him; me writing notes with Wanda looking over my shoulder; and all kinds of single acrobat stunts, or clown-face acts, some pretty good, most pretty dumb.

But *our* pictures weren't what mattered, of course.

Good poses or bad poses, it was what they all had in common that mattered. And that was the figure in the background: the figure of Terry Burch, a tall well-built guy with thick black hair, a sullen mouth, and almost no chin.

By the time we were through, we had two pretty good shots of his face, front and side.

And to make them stand out, Brains ringed them with a white felt marker he'd brought along. Like this:

Shot #1—
Suspect Full-face
(The feet belonged to Willie, who'd been standing on his head.)

Shot #2—
Suspect Side-face
(This time the feet belong to Wanda, who'd been swinging from a tree at the end of the yard.)

"So now," said Brains, as we went over to Wanda's place to work out our next move, "we show the pictures to the girl in Mendoza's store and ask her if she's seen the guy hanging around near there."

"Yeah," said McGurk, grimly. "Or talking to her boss."

But it was already 6:30—far too late to catch Carol at the store. And when we looked in the Griegs' phone book we saw so many different people with the name Rodriguez that even McGurk agreed to call it a day.

"We'll never track her down before bedtime," he said. "But no sweat, men. We'll catch her first thing in the morning, on her way to work."

And this we did.

We caught up with her along Main Street, half a block away from the store.

"Hi!" she said, smiling down at the strained, serious face of McGurk. "What's with you? The watchband bust already? If you think you can get a refund, forget it. Mr. Mendoza would sooner—What's *that?*"

McGurk had flashed his ID card.

"We're on business, Carol. Nothing to do with the watchband. We want your help.

Brains—'' He flicked his fingers. ''Show the lady the mug shots.''

Both Brains and McGurk had brought along magnifying glasses, but they didn't need them.

Carol took one look at the full-face picture and said:

"Hey! Are you *kidding?* This is the jerk that got me into trouble with Mr. Mendoza last month. Over the receipt for the diamond ring."

"You sure?"

"Sure! I'd know that face anywhere!"

We looked at one another. McGurk had gotten pale with excitement. Brains's hand trembled as he held onto the second picture.

"What—what exactly happened, Carol?" Wanda asked.

"Well, he paid by check. And Mr. Mendoza said I should have marked it on the receipt—'Paid by check'—and written its number and everything. Like in case it was phony. Which in this case"—Carol scowled at the man's picture—"I have to admit it was."

"Wow!" said McGurk. "Did you trace the guy? Because we can tell you where—"

"Didn't have to. Mr. Mendoza came back into the store just after I'd finished writing the receipt and was wrapping up the ring. And when old Snakebite Mendoza took a look at the receipt and then at the check, the guy panicked and tried to split. But Mr. Mendoza barred his way."

"Did he call the cops?"

"No. He took the guy into the back room and talked to him a long time. When they came out, Mr. Mendoza was saying, 'O.K.—we'll overlook it this time. But don't ever try that again.' Which surprised me. He's never that soft-hearted when *I* do anything wrong. Not even a small, innocent mistake."

We looked at each other again. I think every one of us, even including Willie, had guessed the reason for the jeweler's soft-heartedness *that* time. You bet! He'd thought of a way to *use* Terry Burch. Someone he'd gotten a hold over. Someone who'd be only too glad to fall in with his scheme. Someone crooked enough, who wouldn't dare snitch on him.

We thanked Carol, and McGurk begged her not to say anything to her boss.

She sniffed.

"Don't *worry!* Who wants to remind that grouch of old mistakes when he's always looking for new ones?"

When she'd gone on her way, we turned to McGurk.

"Well?" said Wanda. "What now?"

"Now we *can* go to Kaspar!" he said.

And he had us run all the way to police headquarters.

12

The Swearing-In of the McGurk Organization

A breeze.

That's what it was, getting Lieutenant Kaspar to listen to us this time. True, as with a lot of breezes, a thundercloud came first.

"Look!" he roared, when we finally got the desk-sergeant to phone through our message, and the lieutenant came storming out, "how many times must I tell you—?"

"But there *is* going to be a robbery, Lieutenant!" said McGurk. "Tonight! We have proof!"

Lieutenant Kaspar sneered.

"Proof! What dumb kid stuff do *you* call proof? Now get out, before—"

"And Terry Burch is involved in it," said McGurk, standing his ground.

The lieutenant stopped in mid-roar, his finger in mid-stab.

"Who?" he said—and his voice was silkily soft now. "What was that name again?"

"Terry Burch."

"You'd better all step into my office," said the lieutenant.

I have to say this much for Lieutenant Kaspar. He may take a lot of convincing, but when he *is* convinced, he's no slouch.

"Well," he said, after we'd told him the whole story and he'd looked up from the evidence we'd laid on his desk—particularly the original note and the receipt—"it looks like you have something after all. And—uh—let me say this here and now: that was a pretty neat piece of detective work."

I thought McGurk might have burst then, he swelled up so fast, like a red balloon. But I guess we were all doing our share of blushing and squirming and smirking, at that.

"*But,*" Lieutenant Kaspar went on, suddenly looking more like his regular mean self, "this is where *your* work ends. From here on in you stay out of this, and you keep quiet about it, until it's all sewed up. Understand?"

McGurk didn't take the hint.

"We *could* stake out Burch's house, Lieutenant," he said eagerly. "And let you know when he leaves. Or—or we could go along to the store and—"

"NO!!" roared Lieutenant Kaspar, halfway out of his chair, stabbing as usual. "This is an official police matter and there's no . . ."

Then he showed that he understood something about kids, after all.

As his voice trailed off, a slow crooked smile began to appear on his face. He sat down. He opened a drawer. He pulled out a book. A black book.

"Come here," he said. "All of you. Put your hands on this Bible. Just a finger will do, so long as you touch it. O.K.? Right! Now say these words after me. . . ."

And so we began, some of us still wondering what was going on.

"As special one-day deputy patrolmen . . ."

"*As special one-day deputy patrolmen . . .*"

". . . we swear . . ."

"*. . . we swear . . .*"

". . . to uphold the law . . ."

"*. . . to uphold the law . . .*"

". . . and obey absolutely . . ."

"*. . . and obey absolutely . . .*"

". . . *all* the orders issued by our superior officers."

"*. . . all the orders issued by our superior officers.*"

And that was it.

We'd been sworn in as deputies!

And as if that wasn't enough, the lieutenant went one better in his determination to keep us out of his hair that evening.

"Which of you is the scientist?" he said.

"I am, sir!" said Brains, standing up straight and saluting.

"You know how to handle a police wave-band radio scanning monitor? Crystal controlled?"

"A what?" whispered Willie.

"Sure do!" said Brains proudly.

"O.K.," said the lieutenant. "We'll loan

you one. We'll get one around to your house early this evening. Then while the stake-out is going on, you'll all be privileged to listen in and hear what happens. Well out of the way.''

I could tell from the look that first crossed McGurk's face that he'd have much preferred to have that special radio in his basement. But after all, Brains was the only one likely to be able to operate it properly. And McGurk was still head-in-the-clouds from being sworn in as a deputy. So:

"Fine!" he said. "We'll have it in our crime lab. Let's just hope that Mr. and Mrs. Bellingham will let us *all* come in and listen."

"Don't worry!" said Lieutenant Kaspar, with what sounded like a sigh of relief. "I'll speak with them personally."

13

The Collar

I'll never forget that evening.

Although we knew the robbery wasn't scheduled until just after nine (fitting the note's description of "as soon as it's really dark"), Wanda, Willie, and I were there with Brains

in the crime lab at 8:30. The room had really
been cleaned up this time, with extra chairs for
us to sit on. The monitor set was on the table
and Brains was having the time of his life,
getting it tuned in.

And at 8:40 we heard the first message from
the stake-out team.

*"Subject is just leaving home now, driving
the red Mustang, number already noted."*

Then came the reply from the Command
Post, in Lieutenant Kaspar's unmistakable
tones.

*"Well, keep a low profile, but don't lose
him."*

Wanda looked around.

"Oh, gosh! This is terrific! But where's
McGurk? He'll miss it *all* if he doesn't hurry!"

I nodded.

It wasn't like McGurk to hold back so long,
I knew. But I also knew how he loves to do
things in style.

"Don't worry," I said. "He's probably been
putting his best suit on. He'll be ready for the
big moment, you can bet on it."

But when nine o'clock came and there was
a report that the red Mustang was slowly proceeding along Main Street, I began to get anxious myself.

"Did he say anything to any of you about being delayed?"

Brains shook his head, then said:

"Shsh! It looks like the action's started!"

From the loudspeaker there came the voice of the first policeman:

"*. . . Mustang is now making a left into Duncan, one block away from jewelry store.*"

Then another voice:

"*This is Charley Baker. We have subject in view in alleyway to rear of store. Mustang is now coming to a stop.*"

Wanda gave a squeak that ended in a groan.

"Oh, it'll all be over by the time he gets here!"

"*Proceed with extreme caution!*" came the lieutenant's voice. "*Do nothing until you receive word from me.*"

There was a sputtering pause. Then:

"*Subject is now leaving car. He is proceeding to rear of building. . . . Now he's trying the yard door, which appears to have been left unlocked. He's going through and—hey!*"

Pause.

"*What? What's wrong, Charley Baker?*"

"*Sir, there must be two of them!*"

"*WHAT?*"

"*Yes, sir! Subject has entered yard and now*"

*a second person—short, under five feet—is
approaching same door. It—it looks like a kid!
He's stopped there and appears to be listening!"*

Wanda turned a chalk-white face.

"Hey! Are you thinking what I'm thinking?"

It was certainly what Lieutenant Kaspar was
thinking.

*"The fool! The young fool! If he goes in
there now he could blow everything. The subject could grab him and hold him as a hostage.
He could get caught in crossfire. He could get
himself killed! . . . Can you head him off without alerting subject?"*

*"Sorry, Lieutenant. The kid has just entered
the yard."*

*"Listen, then. All units. Proceed with ex-
treme caution, but get in there. NOW!"*

We stared at one another, scared, frozen.

All kinds of thoughts were running through
my head.

What if McGurk did get held as hostage?

Or caught in crossfire?

Would his one-day deputy status entitle him
to a big Inspector's Funeral?

What would happen to the Organization after?

Then at last the loudspeaker spit into life again.

"O.K., Lieutenant. Subject apprehended, inside premises. He was immobilizing the alarm."

But Lieutenant Kaspar asked the question we all had on our minds.

"What about the kid?"

"He's O.K. He's here with me now. We caught him peering in through the broken win-

*dow at rear of store. Says his name's McGurk.
I think he's some kind of juvenile nut, Lieutenant. He says—heh! heh!—he says you swore
him in as a deputy, this morning. . . . What
shall I do?''*

Lieutenant Kaspar's voice then came through
loud and clear. And harsh and grating and
chilly as chipped ice:

*"Bring him in with subject. I want a word
with McGurk. And listen—you reading me?''*

"I hear you, sir.''

*"Well, put the cuffs on HIM, too! I've half
a mind to book him on obstruction after all!''*

14

McGurk's Last Case?

But of course Lieutenant Kaspar didn't book McGurk.

What he did do, what he did say to McGurk, I guess we'll never know. McGurk doesn't like to talk about it.

Although I don't think it really bothered him too much, after the first shock.

"I mean I didn't *plan* to go down there," he told us, when we met again next day. "The idea just came to me when I was on my way to the crime lab. I just couldn't resist it." Then a boastful gleam came into his eyes. "But I wouldn't have missed being in at the collar for anything," he said. "Not after all that work I'd put into the case."

"*You'd* put into the case?" we all said, with one mighty roar.

"Well—uh—" He grinned. "With a little help from my staff!"

"And another thing, McGurk," said Wanda. "You ought to be ashamed of yourself. Disobeying Lieutenant Kaspar's order not to go near the store. After you'd sworn on the Bible, too!"

"Not so!" protested McGurk. "That's what *he* said. But as I told him, he gave that order *before* he'd sworn us in. So it didn't count!"

Anyway, it's just as well McGurk did feel good about it, I suppose. Because there was no glory from any court appearance. Terry Burch confessed in full and pleaded guilty, and when that happened Mendoza caved in and did the same. So we didn't have to go and give evidence in court, and the only mention we got in the papers didn't even state our names. Just that the police had acted "on information received."

Which makes this the only true and complete account of The Case of the Secret Scribbler.

"And that's a reward in itself," I said to McGurk, when I told him what I was heading my report.

"Oh? Why?"

"Because for a moment there, that Saturday night, I thought I might have to call it McGurk's Last Case!"

He looked shocked. I think it was the first time the danger had really hit him.

Then slowly a grin spread across his face and he winked and said:

"Don't worry, Joey! *That* won't be for a long time yet!"